STICK MAN

By Julia Donaldson
Illustrated by Axel Scheffler

Arthur A. Levine Books
An Imprint of Scholastic Inc.

Stick Man lives in the family tree
With his Stick Lady Love and their stick children three.

One day he wakes early and goes for a jog.
Stick Man, oh Stick Man, beware of the dog!

"A stick!" barks the dog.
"An excellent stick!
The right kind of stick
for my favorite trick.

"I'll fetch it and drop it,
and fetch it — and then

"I'll drop it and fetch it
and drop it again."

"I'm not a stick! Why can't you see,
I'm Stick Man, *I'm Stick Man*,
I'M STICK MAN, that's me,
And I want to go home to the family tree!"

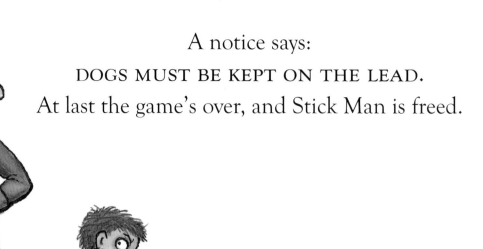

A notice says:
DOGS MUST BE KEPT ON THE LEAD.
At last the game's over, and Stick Man is freed.

He sets off for home with a hop and a twirl.
Stick Man, oh Stick Man, beware of the girl!

"A stick!" cries the girl
with a smile on her face.
"I bet you this stick
will come first in the race!

"Has everyone got one? Get ready to throw."
It's 1, 2, 3 — into the river they go!

"I'm not a stick! Why can't they see,
I'm Stick Man, *I'm Stick Man*, I'M STICK MAN, that's me,
And I'm heading away from the family tree!"

Stick Man is floating. He floats on and on.
Stick Man, oh Stick Man, beware of the swan!

"A twig!" says the swan. "This twig is the best!
It's the right kind of twig to weave into my nest."

"I'm not a twig! Why can't they see,

I'm Stick Man, *I'm Stick Man*, I'M STICK MAN, that's me,

And I long to be back in the family tree."

The nest is deserted, and Stick Man is free.

He drifts down the river and sails out to sea!

He tosses and turns, till the frolicking foam
Washes him up on a beach far from home.

Here comes a dad with a spade in his hand.
Stick Man, oh Stick Man, beware of the sand!

"A mast!" yells the dad. "An excellent mast!

"Hooray! There's a flag on our castle at last."

"I'm not a mast for a silly old flag,

Or a sword for a knight . . .

or a hook for a bag.

I'm not a pen!

I'm not a bow!

I'm not a bat . . .

or a boomerang — no, I'm . . ."

Stick Man, oh Stick Man, beware of the snow!

Here comes a boy in a warm woolly scarf.
"An arm for my snowman!" he says with a laugh.

"I'M NOT AN ARM! Can nobody see,
I'm Stick Man, *I'm Stick Man*, I'M STICK MAN, that's me!

"Will I *ever* get back to the family tree?"

Stick Man is lonely, Stick Man is lost.
Stick Man is frozen and covered in frost.
Stick Man is weary. His eyes start to close.
He stretches and yawns and lies down for a doze.

He can't hear the bells, or the sweet-singing choir . . .

Or the voice saying, "Here's a good stick for the fire!"

Stick Man is lying asleep in the grate.

Can anyone wake him before it's too late?

He dreams of his kids and his Stick Lady Love,

Then suddenly wakes.
What's that noise up above?
It starts as a chuckle,
then turns to a shout:
"Oh-ho-ho ho-ho . . . I'm STUCK!
Get me OUT!"

A Stuck Man? *A Stuck Man?*
Now who could that be?
"Don't worry!" cries Stick Man.
"I'll soon set you free."

A scratch and a scrape and
a flurry of soot.
A wiggle, a jiggle, and —
out pokes a foot!
A shove and a nudge,
a hop and a jump . . .

And Santa falls into the room with a thump!

"Stick Man, oh Stick Man, you excellent friend!
Thanks! Thanks a million! Thanks without end!"

Then Stick Man helps Santa deliver the toys
To fast-asleep girls . . .

and to fast-asleep boys.

Faster and faster they fly through the snow,
Till Santa says, "Only one chimney to go!"

Stick Lady's lonely. The children are sad.
It won't feel like Christmas without their Stick Dad.
They toss and they turn in the family bed.
But what is that clattering sound overhead?

Someone is tumbling into their house.
Is it a bird, or a bat, or a mouse?
Or could it . . . yes, could it just possibly be . . .

"I'm Stick Man, *I'm Stick Man,*
I'M STICK MAN, that's me!
And I'm sticking right here
in the family tree."

For Adélie

Text copyright © 2008 by Julia Donaldson
Illustrations copyright © 2008 by Axel Scheffler

All rights reserved. Published by Arthur A. Levine Books, an imprint of Scholastic Inc.,
Publishers since 1920, by arrangement with Scholastic Children's Books, London, England.
SCHOLASTIC, the LANTERN LOGO, and associated logos are trademarks and/or
registered trademarks of Scholastic Inc.

The Library of Congress has cataloged the jacketed hardcover edition as follows:
Donaldson, Julia. Stick Man / by Julia Donaldson ; illustrated by Axel Scheffler. — 1st American ed.   p. cm.
Summary: Stick Man ends up far away from his family tree when he is fetched by a dog, thrown by a child, used as a snowman's
arm, and even put on a fire, but finally Santa Claus steps in to make sure that Stick Man and his family have a joyous Christmas.
ISBN-13: 978-0-545-15761-2 • ISBN-10: 0-545-15761-7 (hardcover : alk. paper)
[1. Stories in rhyme. 2. Twigs—Fiction. 3. Santa Claus—Fiction.] I. Scheffler, Axel, ill. II. Title.
PZ8.3.D7235St 2009 • [E] —dc22
2008048323

33614057811753

ISBN 978-0-545-94789-3

10 9 8 7 6 5 4 3 2 1   16 17 18 19 20

Printed in Malaysia
This edition first printing October 2016